INNCONVENIENT MURDER

SIT, STAY, SLEEP COZY MYSTERIES
BOOK 1

PATTI BENNING

SUMMER PRESCOTT BOOKS PUBLISHING

Copyright 2025 Summer Prescott Books

All Rights Reserved. No part of this publication nor any of the information herein may be quoted from, nor reproduced, in any form, including but not limited to: printing, scanning, photocopying, or any other printed, digital, or audio formats, without prior express written consent of the copyright holder.

**This book is a work of fiction. Any similarities to persons, living or dead, places of business, or situations past or present, is completely unintentional.

CHAPTER ONE

"It looks like we just passed the turn into town. See? I told you we wouldn't be too far out in the middle of nowhere."

Sadie Barton watched the overgrown wooden sign with the faded words, *Welcome to Greencreek!* shrink in her rearview mirror. It was the first sign of civilization she had seen for at least half an hour. In the backseat, her foxhound, Jasper, had his nose pressed to the window, leaving a new smudge each time he readjusted. They had left Lexington eight and a half hours ago, and his enthusiasm hadn't waned once. Even Penny, who was driving her little red crossover down the road in front of Sadie's larger SUV, had gone quiet for a few hours somewhere between Knoxville and Chattanooga.

Sadie's own enthusiasm had waned at about the same time as she saw the reality of her empty bank account, but there was no turning back now.

"We are in the middle of nowhere, Penny. The town's just stuck out here with us. We're a two-hour drive away from the closest city."

"Don't be a downer. You sound like a spoiled city girl."

Sadie rolled her eyes at her friend's voice, which floated clearly over her SUV's speakers. They had been chatting for the past hour, more in an effort to make sure they didn't get lost when they got off the freeway than out of any need to stay awake. Sadie hadn't slept right since the day they closed. She was too hyped up on nerves and caffeine to worry about drifting off behind the wheel now.

"I am a spoiled city girl. So are you. Jasper's the only one who's got a hint of country in him, and I think I've spoiled most of that out of him by now, too. He's used to air conditioning and filtered water. The poor guy is going to wonder what he did wrong when he sees where we're going to live."

"He's going to love it, and the two of us will adapt," Penny replied. "Come on, cheer up. This is the beginning of the greatest adventure of our lives. We're almost there."

Ahead of her, the red crossover's brake lights came on. This was concerning, because the road ahead of them didn't look any different than the last fifteen miles had, with thick, green forest on both sides. The trees were heavy with kudzu, an invasive vine that seemed to take over more and more of the landscape the farther south they went. Penny's left turn blinker came on. Sadie slowed further, finally spotting the turnoff, though what she didn't see was the sign for the motel that had been in the listing photos.

"Are you sure this is the right place?" she asked as she hit her own turn signal, cognizant of the rented trailer behind her as she slowed. They had stuffed as many of their possessions inside as would fit and put the rest in a shared storage unit up in Lexington, with vague plans to bring it down during their next visit home.

She hoped against hope that Penny had typed the wrong address into her phone, but she had a sinking feeling that this was the right place. The property was more overgrown than it had looked in the photos, but there was the L-shaped building they had spent their combined life savings on: a run-down, ten room motel with eight indoor-outdoor dog kennels out back and a few outbuildings that were listed as *Enter at your own risk* online. Ten acres all told, and dirt cheap for what it was.

The price was the first red flag they had chosen to ignore.

The second red flag was the article their real estate agent had forwarded to them about a string of bloody murders that had taken place at the motel two years ago.

In retrospect, the third was probably the fact that their agent had pushed them to buy the property sight-unseen, claiming it would get snatched up quickly if they dawdled.

"This is it," Penny said unnecessarily as she parked on the cracked remnants of what had once been a nice asphalt parking lot but was now almost as overgrown as the rest of the property. "I'm sure it's not as bad as it looks. Let's check things out, then head into town to grab some food before it gets dark."

Sadie grabbed Jasper's leash as she got out of her SUV. His training had come along in leaps and strides since she adopted him a year ago, but the last thing she needed was for him to take off running in a moment of rebellion in a place they were both unfamiliar with. She was also more than a little concerned about what exactly they would find when they explored the building. Broken glass, rat poison… nothing seemed out of the realm of possibility.

The heat and humidity were the first things that hit her when she got out of her SUV. She felt like she was trying to breathe in water. Kentucky in mid-August could get pretty brutal, but an eight-hour drive south to Georgia was enough to make her miss Kentucky's weather instantly.

The smell was the second thing: the air smelled *green*, of both growing things and dying things. Insects buzzed and hummed in the kudzu-draped trees all around them, but beneath the steady drone was a silence she had never experienced in the city.

Jasper was thrilled when she clipped the leash to his collar, unclasped the seat belt attachment from his harness, and let him out of the vehicle. He had his nose to the ground in an instant, exploring a world of scent that she could only imagine.

"It's going to need some elbow grease, but I bet the interior looks better," Penny said as she walked over to join Sadie and Jasper. She fished a key ring out of the packet their real estate's proxy had given them at closing. It had a lot of keys on it. Apparently, each of the rooms was keyed separately. "Where do you want to start?"

Sadie was tempted to suggest they start with the

kennels, since that was the part she was the most excited for. The promise of finally having her own dog boarding and training business was what had kept her going on the long drive down from Lexington, and before that too.

But the kennels were around back, and the kennels weren't where they were planning on sleeping tonight. It made the most sense to check out the motel itself first, in case they needed to make other arrangements.

"Let's start with the lobby and work our way down the rooms," she suggested.

Penny nodded, and the three of them walked over to the lobby at the front corner of the building. The door was painted a dingy white, the paint peeling to reveal rusting metal beneath, and the windows had been covered with plywood panels that had already begun to rot away in the humidity. There was no overhang, so the sun beat down on them while Penny tried keys in the lock. By the time she found the right one, Sadie was sweating, and poor Jasper was panting.

The door creaked open beneath Penny's manicured hand. She walked inside fearlessly. Sadie followed, telling herself the musty smell that wafted out of the dark building was just mildew, not mold.

"Where's the light switch? It's got to be somewhere…" Penny murmured. Sadie heard her slapping the wall, though she was temporarily blinded as her eyes adjusted to going from brutal sunlight to darkness in the space of a single step.

She heard a click, and the lobby filled with dim yellow light. Jasper was already sniffing the stained Berber carpet. She pulled him back and kept his leash short as she stepped further into the room.

The lobby was small, with about two-thirds of the wall to their right taken up by a long, heavy desk. There was a plexiglass partition to keep guests away from whoever was working behind the service desk, and a very solid looking door that blocked the space behind the desk off from the rest of the room completely. A small window would give the person behind the desk some fresh air, and there was a hatch that led to a drop box Sadie had seen outside for key returns.

At the far end of the desk, there was a door set into the wall that supposedly led to the stairs up to the small apartment that the listing had boasted. In the corner, an ancient tube TV hung above a long-deceased potted plant. A row of uncomfortable looking chairs was set up along the other wall, along with a full garbage can and an empty water cooler. The wall at the far end of the room held another door.

This one led to the back half of the L-shaped building, which held the laundry room and kennels. A few of the panels on the drop ceiling were stained. Sadie saw some matching stains on the carpet beneath those spots. She just hoped the leaks weren't too bad, because they didn't have a full roof replacement in the budget right now.

"It's got promise," Penny said with the same good cheer that had kept them both going since she sent Sadie the listing three months ago. "It'll look a lot better once we take that plywood down and let some sunlight in here. We'll have to take that plexiglass down too, or I'm going to feel like a goldfish in a bowl while I'm checking our guests in."

"I think we should wait on the plexiglass," Sadie said. "The previous owner might have installed it for a reason. We should tear the carpet out first thing. I think that's where most of the smell is coming from."

They would want an easy to clean hard floor for her canine clients. She just had to focus on what they were working towards; a motel for Penny to run, where she could put all of her experience as manager of a chain hotel to good use, and Sadie's boarding and training kennel, which would cater to guests who wanted a safe place to leave their pets during the day while they enjoyed their vacation. She hoped they would get a lot of local clients, too. They had done their research, and there weren't many other boarding kennels in the area.

"Right, we tear down the plywood first, then start on the carpet." Penny turned around to face Sadie, her grin undaunted. "We'll tear a corner up tomorrow and see what's underneath and what we have to work wi…"

She broke off with a shriek and jumped backwards, her gaze fixed on something behind Sadie. Sadie spun around to find a man with untrimmed hair that fell past his ears and scruffy facial hair standing in the doorway. Her eyes only lingered on his features for a second before they fixed on the bright red fireman's axe in his hands.

That was when she started to scream, too.

CHAPTER TWO

Sadie stumbled backwards until she felt Penny grab her elbow. In the space of a few moments, her friend yanked both of them, and Jasper too, through the heavy door that led to the plexiglass-encased room behind the desk. As soon as Jasper's tail was through, Sadie slammed the door shut and engaged the lock. Her dog, whom she could lovingly describe as dumb as a box of rocks, placed his front paws on the desk and wagged his tail as he looked out at the axe-murderer, his pink tongue lolling happily out of his mouth.

The axe-murderer walked over to them, each step slow and measured as if he enjoyed their terror.

"Oh my God, oh my God, we're going to die," Penny shrieked, clinging to Sadie's arm. Sadie was frozen. Even if she wanted to, she couldn't have forced her fingers to uncurl from where they were clinging to Jasper's leather leash. In some quiet corner of her mind, she was aware that they should be calling the police, but she had left her phone in her car, and she was pretty sure Penny had, too.

The axe-murderer stopped in front of the desk and shifted his grip on the axe to one hand so he could rap on the glass with the knuckles of his other hand. Penny went silent, but her grip on Sadie's arm only tightened. Once he knew he had their attention, he jerked his head toward the door and gestured pointedly to indicate they should open it.

Sadie shook her head frantically. Penny let out a high-pitched sound of pure terror. The man, who looked like he lived in the woods and probably used his axe to murder people on the regular, gave them a scowl filled with such sheer exasperation that Sadie was surprised they didn't drop dead from the look alone.

Then he turned on his heel and strode out of the building without saying a word. Sadie and Penny stood frozen for long seconds after he had gone.

"Did… did he give up?" her friend whispered at last.

"I don't know," Sadie whispered back. "I thought

you said they caught the killer from those murders a couple years ago."

"They did!" Penny hissed. "The guy's behind bars. Thirty-five to life."

"Well, they obviously got the wrong guy!"

"Maybe he's just a local who decided to prank us. I mean, he could have killed us, but he didn't. That's a good sign, right?"

The squabbling was grounding. She and Penny had been best friends since middle school. They were more like sisters sometimes, really. Talking to her was as familiar as breathing, and it made it easier for Sadie to think.

"I'm not about to bet my life on it being a prank," she said. "He might be waiting for us outside. We could go out through the kennels and try to sneak around the building to one of our cars."

"Shoot, what if he steals all of our stuff? Did you bring your keys in?"

She hadn't, but it didn't matter, because at that moment, the man returned. Except this time, he was carrying a yellow legal pad and a pen instead of his axe. When he saw that they were still huddled behind the desk, he gave them an annoyed look and scribbled something on the pad of paper, which he then slapped face-first against the plexiglass.

What are you doing here?

"What are we doing here?" Penny said, her voice high-pitched. "We aren't the ones threatening people with an axe!"

"We're the new owners," Sadie said, a little calmer. She figured the axe being gone was probably a good sign.

The man raised an eyebrow, clearly skeptical. She wondered why he wouldn't talk to them. Was it an intimidation tactic? If so, it was working.

Proof, or I call the cops, was his next scribbled message.

Penny was the one who froze this time, so Sadie nudged her with her elbow until her friend jumped and opened the packet they had gotten at the title company when they closed; the packet she was still carrying.

"I don't know what counts as proof, but here. Look. We signed for the title, and we have keys. Here's the printout of the listing. Oh, and a receipt for the wire transfer…" Penny was babbling. The man's eyes were a light hazel, she noticed. It made him look a little like a werewolf when paired with the scruffy hair and general mountain man vibes. He skimmed over the papers as Penny held them up one after another. Finally, he gestured for her to stop and bent to scribble on his pad again. Sadie inched closer to the plexiglass, curious.

I believe you. Sorry for startling you. Thought you had broken in.

Sadie snorted. Startled? More like terrified them half to death. Penny let out a laugh that rang out a little too high-pitched. The man glanced at the door again, waiting.

Sadie exchanged a look with her friend, a lifetime of experience getting into trouble together in that single, wordless exchange. There was no way either one of them was opening that door, not yet.

"Who are you?" Sadie asked instead of reaching for the lock.

He wrote something on his notepad, paused briefly, added something else, then held it up. *Sam Walker. Your tenant.*

She exchanged another look with Penny, this one confused. Her friend looked just as clueless as her. After a second, she began thumbing through the packet again. While Penny tried to find verification, Sadie turned back to Sam. He was a little less intimidating now that he wasn't carrying an axe and she knew his name, but she didn't remember hearing anything about a tenant.

"You live in the motel?" she asked.

He shook his head and wrote, *House on the property.*

"There's a house on the property?"

"Here it is," Penny said before he could answer. She withdrew a paper and read it quickly, her eyes flicking across the photocopy. "It's a lease with his name on it, all right. A five-year lease. Signed a year ago."

She gave Sadie a meaningful look, one she tried hard not to grimace at. Four years left with a tenant who liked to surprise people with an axe didn't sound ideal. She didn't know much about the laws surrounding tenants and landlords, but she was pretty sure they couldn't evict someone just because they bought the property. Rental agreements carried over with sales like this, didn't they?

"What does this mean? We can't use the motel?" she asked, a different sort of panic beginning to set in.

"No, I don't think that'll be an issue," Penny said, her brow furrowing as she scrutinized the lease agreement. "It looks like whatever building he's renting has its own address. It's Mailbox A and we're Mailbox B. I guess we're, like, landlords now?"

She looked at Sadie with an expression that was as befuddled as Sadie felt. Landlords for a tenant they hadn't known existed, who was renting a house they hadn't known existed. She tried to look on the bright side.

"Does that mean we're getting rental income?"

A hopeful look flashed across Penny's face. She looked back down at the lease agreement. The expression dimmed a little. "We are... but it's only five-hundred dollars a month. It's probably been going into an escrow account since we closed, unless the old owner never set that up, in which case he owes us a thousand bucks."

Five-hundred dollars a month wasn't much, but it was something, especially since they didn't exactly have other income right now. They had managed to scrape together enough to pay for the property in cash. A necessity, since it had been a cash-only sale. So, on the upside, they didn't have any recurring expenses either. Sadie's SUV was paid off, and she knew Penny's parents still covered her car payment. Penny's family wasn't filthy rich, but they were close. Sadie, who had grown up solidly middle-class, had long since come to terms with the fact that her best friend simply didn't see money the same way she did. Penny made an effort to be independent from her family, but she knew help was just a phone call away. Sadie had no such financial padding to rely on.

Just buying the property had nearly cleaned them

out. They had drained most of their savings and the lawsuit settlement Penny had gotten when a city-owned bus hit her while she was crossing the street a few years ago and had just enough left over to support themselves and pay for some basic repairs and updates for the next couple of months. If that ran out before they began bringing in money, they would have to rely on loans to keep them going… or give the whole thing up as a bad idea and sell the motel for whatever they could get for it.

When Sadie finally glanced back at Sam, he was standing with his arms crossed, clearly impatient. They were being rude, she realized, talking about him as if he wasn't there. According to the paper Penny was still clutching, he really was their tenant, which meant they didn't have much choice but to trust him since they were stuck with him for the next four years.

Unless he had killed the real Sam Walker and was lying as a ploy to lure them out where he could proceed to axe-murder them at his leisure.

She swallowed and glanced down at Jasper. He had given up at looking at Sam through the window and was sniffing at the remnants of a mouse nest on the floor. She wanted to take his lack of concern as a good sign, but Jasper had never met a person he didn't like, and she didn't expect him to start with this man even if he was a serial killer.

Would he try to defend them if Sam turned out to be a bad guy? She had no idea, but at least he was a big dog, and Sam didn't know he was about as likely to bite as an earthworm was.

She took a breath and turned the lock on the doorknob. She felt Penny go still beside her but didn't look back at her friend. They couldn't stay stuck in here forever. At some point, they were going to have to go out there and make their peace with Sam, and she had never been one to put off the inevitable.

She left the plexiglass fishbowl and stepped around the front desk, extending her hand toward Sam in an effort to get the encounter back to something resembling normalcy.

"It's nice to meet you, Sam. I'm Sadie Barton, and the woman who just locked me out here with you is my best friend, Penelope Montgomery. We just moved from Lexington, and we're here to reopen the motel."

CHAPTER THREE

Sam eyed her hand for a long moment before he finally shook it. He released her hand nearly as soon as he took it, then glanced at Penny through the glass. Sadie turned toward her too, placing her hands on her hips as she raised her eyebrows. She saw her friend's shoulders slump. A moment later, she unlocked the door and cautiously walked out into the main area of the lobby.

"So... we aren't being murdered?"

"It doesn't seem that way," Sadie said. Turning back to Sam, who was leaning down to pat Jasper, she said, "Where do you live, exactly? We had no idea there was a house on the property. Or that someone lived there."

He straightened up and jerked his head toward the

door. As he turned away, clearly expecting them to follow him, Sadie exchanged another glance with Penny. Her friend still looked like she was halfway terrified and shook her head minutely. It was clear she didn't think they should trust this guy enough to follow him into the unknown.

Sadie weighed the thought of possibly offending their surprise tenant against the risk of being murdered and decided that the latter wasn't all that likely. After all, he had put the axe down instead of using it to hack through the door. If he wanted to hurt them, he could have done it without luring them out first.

She patted her friend's arm in reassurance, then took a step toward Sam before hesitating again. "Hold on," she said. "Why won't you talk to us?"

He scribbled on his notepad, a single word, then held it up. *Mute.*

She was curious, but she knew it was bad manners to ask too many questions about someone's disability. With Jasper's leash still clutched tightly in her hand, she followed Sam outside. Out of the dim, musty lobby, everything seemed a little less frightening, including Sam. She spotted the axe leaning against the wall of the motel. Sam followed her glance toward it but didn't make a move to pick it up. Penny trailed behind Sadie, letting out a nervous laugh as she backed toward her crossover.

"I'm just going to grab my phone," she said. "Sadie, didn't you say you wanted to get something out of your purse?"

It only took Sadie a second to decipher her friend's pointed look. She carried a small canister of pepper spray in her purse for her late night walks with Jasper. It wouldn't hurt to grab it… just in case.

"That's right," she said. "Just one second."

She gave Sam a tight smile, then hurried over to her SUV, where she dug through her purse for her keys, her phone, and her pepper spray. She slipped the latter into her shorts pocket discreetly, then locked her vehicle. Penny was standing by her crossover, clutching her phone like a lifeline. Sam watched them both warily, like *they* were the ones who had surprised *him* with an axe. When he saw they were ready, he jerked his head towards the northern edge of the property. There was a narrow trail through the long grass. It didn't look like much more than a game trail, and Sadie would never have guessed that it led to a small, yellow house that was hidden at the end of a long, dirt driveway, out of sight of the road. Though old, the house was clearly well-cared for. Unlike the overgrown area surrounding the motel, the yard was trimmed and tidy. There was a small vegetable garden, a clothesline, and a fire pit with a couple folding chairs set up around a metal ring. An old pickup truck was parked in the shade under a tall tree.

"Huh," Penny said. "There really is a house."

Sam gave her a *what did you expect* look. Sadie looked around, pleasantly surprised. No, having a surprise tenant wasn't ideal, and they could probably get more rent than Sam was paying if they weren't locked into the lease with him… and said lease meant neither of them could actually use this house, but it wasn't all bad. They had some passive income, even if it was only a small amount, and it was reassuring to see that something on this property was in good condition.

"It's a nice place," Sadie said. She wondered how much else had been conveniently skipped over during the rushed sale. "It was, um, nice to meet you, Sam. Penny and I need to go finish looking over the motel, but we should probably meet with you in the next couple of days to talk… uh, communicate about how this is going to work. Neither of us knows the first thing about being landlords."

I'll be around; he wrote on the notepad.

She nodded once and, with an awkward smile,

retreated back down the game trail and out of sight with Jasper at her side and Penny close behind.

"What the *heck*?" her friend hissed as soon as they were out of earshot. "How did our agent leave out the fact that we've got some random guy living on the property?"

"I don't know," Sadie replied. "He didn't mention the house either. You know, I bet that raises the property value. We might not be completely out of luck if we have to resell this place."

"You're not thinking of giving up already, are you? I thought you were just as excited about this as I am. You've been talking about opening your own training business for years."

"I know," Sadia said. "And I am. Really. I'm just also terrified, and the motel is going to need a lot more work than we expected."

"We can do it," Penny said with a confidence Sadie felt was unearned. Neither of them was exactly flush with handyman skills. "It might take a little longer to open than we hoped, but we'll manage. You'll see."

Sadie made a doubtful sound. They reached the end of the little trail that led to Sam's house and the motel came into view again. She tried to see the promise in it that Penny did, but all she saw was a mistake.

Sam left them alone while they explored the rest of the building, but his sudden appearance with the axe had soured the mood somewhat, and they moved through first the motel, then the kennels quickly. The little apartment tucked away above the lobby was still cluttered with the previous owner's possessions and smelled like potpourri and old people. The rooms themselves weren't too bad. As musty and dated as the lobby was, the building seemed to be structurally sound, at least. The tenth and last room was the exception. Faded crime scene tape streamed from the doorknob, and when Sadie turned the knob to find the room a mess, with a missing mattress and mysterious rusty spots on the carpet, she put the pieces together quickly enough.

"Nope." She shut the door before Penny could get a look. Her friend wasn't good with blood or violence of any sort. "We'll deal with this one later."

"Why? What's wrong?"

"I'm pretty sure that's the room where the murders happened."

Her friend's blue eyes went wide. "Don't say more. I don't want the details. Let's go look at the kennels."

They walked around to the back of the building to look at the outdoor runs first. Like everything else, they were overgrown, but Sadie was relieved to see that the chain link all looked like it was in good condition. She would need to spend some time pulling weeds and grass out of the pea gravel inside of the runs. She didn't like the thought of using chemical weed killer in a dog run, even if it claimed it was pet safe, but they should be usable with only a few hours' worth of work.

It was the interior that she was more worried about. The back door was locked with a rusted padlock, which Penny thankfully had a key for. She unlocked it, then stepped back and let Sadie go first. This part of the building was going to be her realm. Her baby. Her part of the business to make or break.

Each of the eight runs was indoor-outdoor, with a doggy door between the interior and exterior. There was a four or five foot wide hallway that led down past the row of kennels and back toward the front corner of the building where the lobby was. Sadie was relieved to discover that the kennels were in much better shape than the lobby and motel rooms were. It probably helped that there were no carpets in here to get musty. The floors were lacquered with a pale blue epoxy that wouldn't need much more than a good mopping to get clean. Jasper sniffed at dust bunnies in a corner while she peered into the kennels. They were spacious enough for large dogs, but secure enough for small ones. Like the rest of the building, someone had nailed plywood over the windows, but the fluorescent lights lit the room up nicely, though she suspected the buzz from the bulbs would drive both her and the dogs crazy if she didn't replace them.

The kennel room was hot and stuffy, but after some poking and prodding, she got the ancient, wall-mounted air conditioning unit to come to life.

"This is the nicest part of the whole building," Penny said. "Lucky. You'll be able to keep us afloat with boarding and training while we fix the rest of the place up."

"We should start marketing right away," Sadie said. "If we get the rest of the property cleaned up or at least trim the grass, get rid of the weeds on the parking lot and put a sign up so people know where to turn in, I could probably get everything ready to start accepting boarding clients in a week."

They had already prepared their business licenses and insurance. There were a few more formalities they had to get through now that they were finally at the property in person, including an inspection of the boarding facilities, but if they put the work in, she thought a week to begin taking boarding clients was realistic, even if it wouldn't be easy.

"A week," Penny murmured. "This is actually happening. It finally feels real."

Sadie exchanged a smile with her friend. She was still terrified that purchasing the motel had been a mistake but seeing the kennels… it made the fear fade a little.

The laundry room was the last room they toured: two industrial sized washers and dryers would be invaluable for keeping up with cleaning, and there was plenty of space to store other supplies. It was well into evening by the time they finished their inspection of the property, an inspection they should have done before they bought it, but having seen the whole thing, Sadie felt a little better.

It was going to be hard work, but Penny was right. They could do this.

CHAPTER FOUR

They were both exhausted from their long drive down from Kentucky, but they still had to make a run into town before bed, so after cleaning out one of the kennels for Jasper and getting him settled inside with his bed, some fresh water, and his dinner, she left him there with the air conditioning cranked so he could get some rest while she and Penny ran to the store.

The store which closed at eight. They made it with only ten minutes to spare and had to race to the register with their haul of microwaveable food when the last call came over the intercom.

"Are you two from out of town?" the young woman who rang them up asked. Her name tag read *Elena.*

"We're from Kentucky," Sadie explained. "We just moved here."

"We're reopening that motel on Highway 78," Penny added. "We're going to offer dog training and boarding, too. Sadie's a great trainer. We're thinking of doing an open house soon. Do you think people would come?"

Elena perked up a little, polite curiosity turning to something a little more genuine. "Definitely. I don't know if you know, but that place has a history. I know a lot of people who have a morbid fascination with it. You know, we have a bulletin board by the door. You can pin the information about the open house up there if you want. It's free for anyone to use."

"Oh, that's great to know," Penny said as she tucked her card back into her purse. "Thanks!"

"Good luck," Elena said. Sadie thought she heard her add a muttered, *"You're going to need it,"* as they walked away, but when she glanced back, the younger woman had her back turned and was wiping down her register.

"Okay, no more middle of the night grocery runs," Penny said as they loaded their groceries into her crossover. "That's fine."

Sadie grinned as she tossed a box of crackers into

the back. "Are you sure? Because you sound like it's not fine."

"Eight is so early to close. Ten? That would be reasonable. But eight? Is everyone around here in bed by nine?"

Sadie let her friend rant while she returned the cart. She got into the passenger seat and cranked the air conditioning while Penny climbed into the driver's seat.

"Where to next? Do you want to explore a little, or should we head straight back?"

Sadie wanted to check on Jasper, but she was curious about their new town, too. Greencreek, Georgia was small enough that it barely had an online presence. It was the sort of sleepy southern town she had always seen in movies but never thought actually existed.

"Let's cruise down Main Street and see what stores there are," she suggested. "I doubt anything will be open, but we can come back tomorrow to check out anything that looks interesting."

Penny nodded and backed out of their spot. Main Street was all but dead, except for a busy parking lot at the far end of town which turned out to belong to the local bar. Neither of them felt like exploring the local bar scene after their long day, so Penny turned around to drive them slowly back down Main Street.

They passed a hardware store that Sadie had a feeling they were going to be seeing a lot of, a couple of small boutique stores, a hair salon, a diner, and a handful of closed storefronts. Everything was closed until they reached a dessert shop. The sign, which read *Sunshine Desserts* and was done up in pastels with stylized images of cookies and cakes, stood out as a burst of color, and someone was carrying a gift basket of cookies out of the store to load them into a small, white delivery van. The neon sign in the window still flashed *Open*. A young man wearing a backwards baseball cap with a skateboard propped up next to him leaned against the wall, fiddling with his phone.

A glance was all it took to silently confirm that they were on the same page. Penny parallel parked in front of the delivery van. It was an easy feat, considering no one else was parked along the street, and they got out of the crossover together.

They were halfway to the dessert shop's entrance when the young woman hopped down from the delivery van and said, "I'm so sorry, we're actually closed. I forgot to shut the sign off."

"Oh." Sadie exchanged a disappointed glance

with Penny. "That's okay. We'll come back tomorrow."

The young man glanced up from his phone briefly but didn't seem to care about them and quickly returned to whatever he was scrolling through. The woman looked them over, her gaze curious.

"Are y'all visiting from out of town?"

"You're the second person who has pegged us as newcomers," Penny said. "Do we stand out that badly?"

The woman glanced at the shiny red crossover behind them, then turned to look at the dessert shop. "You could say that. Locals would know we closed at six. Why don't y'all come in anyway? I'm happy to sell you anything you want out of the display cases. I already zeroed out the card machine for the day, so you'll have to pay in cash."

"Cash works," Penny said cheerfully. "Thanks so much."

"Seriously?" the young man grumbled. "I've got plans tonight, Bailey."

"It'll take five minutes. And we only have a few orders to drop off. Just hang tight." She followed them inside. As the door swung shut behind them, she said, "Sorry about Josh. I keep telling him he has to be nicer to customers."

"It's fine," Sadie said. "We're bothering you when you're technically closed, after all. Ooh, you sell dog treats?"

As soon as she saw the display case, everything else was forgotten. She peered through the glass at the peanut butter, bacon, and vanilla flavored cookies under the sign that read *Cookies for Dogs!*

"Those are popular," Bailey said with a smile. "Do you two have dogs?"

"She has a foxhound," Penny said, jabbing her thumb over her shoulder at Sadie as she examined the offerings intended for human consumption. "He's a dork, but he loves everyone. Even axe-wielding maniacs."

Sadie finally tore herself away from the display case so she could see what else the little shop offered. "He's not a maniac. He thought we were breaking in. He was just going to scare us off." She paused. "Probably."

Bailey's eyebrows rose in a manicured arch. "This sounds like an interesting story."

"It was just a… misunderstanding," Sadie said. "We just bought that motel on Highway 78, and our tenant surprised us. It turned out he was just looking after the property."

"Oh, Sam?" Bailey said. "Yeah, he's a bit strange,

but he's harmless. The two of you are the ones who bought Walter Bennington's old place? I heard it sold, but I thought a corporation bought it. I figured they'd knock it down and put a gas station in or something. What are you going to do with the place?"

"We're hoping to reopen it," Sadie told her.

Penny came over to stand next to her. "We're going to do a sort of dog motel. We'll offer boarding and daycare and training since it's already got some nice kennels out back in addition to the motel basics."

"I see," Bailey said. Her smile no longer quite reached her eyes. "Well... good luck. It sounds like you could use some sugar to fuel all the work you have ahead of you. What can I get you?"

They left Sunshine Desserts with two bags, one full of human cookies, and the other full of the canine version. Sadie hoped Jasper gave them his seal of approval, because she was already toying with the idea of asking Bailey if she would be willing to sell some of her dog cookies at the kennel once they opened.

"I think Room Three is in the best shape," Penny said as they left town, and she turned onto the state highway. "It has those two queen sized beds in it. I figure we can strip the bedding, turn the mattresses over, and put our own bedding on instead. We can tear those plywood panels down and let the room air out a little while we eat. That should get us through the night, and tomorrow we can start cleaning that little apartment out for you."

"Are you sure you're okay with staying in one of the rooms until you find somewhere to rent?" Sadie asked. "I already feel bad that I'm taking the apartment."

"I told you, it's fine," her friend said as she slowed for the turn into the motel's parking lot. "It makes sense for you to get the apartment that's on-site, since you'll have dogs boarding in the kennels soon and you'll want to be here overnight in case something happens. That means I won't be the one the guests complain to in the middle of the night; sounds like a good deal to me. I'll find a room or a studio apartment to rent in the next couple of weeks, but I can rough it in a motel room for now."

They would both be roughing it for a while. The place needed a lot of work, but at least so far it seemed like everything essential was functional. She took both bags of cookies with her when she got out of the crossover.

"I'm going to go offer Sam one of these to try and make up for earlier," she said. "I'll help you get started on Room Three when I get back."

"He's the one who showed up with an axe," Penny said. "What are you apologizing for?"

"For not even knowing we had a tenant, I guess," Sadie said. "I mean, I wasn't planning on becoming a landlord, but now that I am, I want to be a good one, you know? The whole thing was just… awkward, and I want to smooth it over if I can."

"Well, all right," Penny said doubtfully. "Be careful. I know that woman from the cookie shop, Bailey, said he was harmless, but plenty of people thought that about serial killers until they were caught."

"It'll be fine," Sadie said. "I think it really was all just a misunderstanding. But if I disappear, you know who to blame."

Her friend sighed and held out a manicured hand. Her nail polish was red. It was her go-to color for everything, even her hair. "Fine. Give me the dog treats, I'll take one to Jasper and tell him his owner abandoned him for a mountain man."

She handed the bag over. "Let me know if he likes it. I'm thinking we can sell the cookies, both dog and human, to our guests if they taste as good as they look."

They went their separate ways, Penny inside the motel and Sadie back down the overgrown trail between the motel and Sam's house. She tried not to think about ticks as the tall grass tickled her legs. Yard care wasn't just aesthetic, it would also help keep the bugs down, too. They needed to get serious about it before their open house, but the fact that they didn't even have a mower was going to make things difficult.

As she reached the end of the trail and scanned Sam's yard, her eyes narrowed. There was a shed, maybe more of a lean-to, at the far edge of the lawn, with a nice-looking mower and a few other tools. They might not have the right equipment to tame the jungle that had grown up around the motel in two years of neglect, but their tenant slash neighbor did.

Now even more glad that she had brought cookies, she marched up the steps to his porch and raised a fist, but the storm door swung open before her knuckles made contact. Sam had showered at some point since she last saw him and looked a little more presentable. He made some sort of motion with his hands. *Sign language*, she thought. She had never had occasion to regret not learning it before. It had been between that, Spanish, and German in her first year of college, and Spanish had seemed the most useful at the time.

"I brought cookies as a peace offering," she said raising the bag. "And a proposal."

CHAPTER FIVE

In exchange for a month's rent, Sam agreed to help them clean up the motel's lawn and the kennels. They hadn't been expecting the rental income anyway, so Sadie figured it wasn't much of a loss, and Sam proved invaluable. In fact, she suspected she and Penny had gotten the better end of the deal, though he didn't complain about the long hours of work he put in. He certainly seemed a lot less bothered by the heat than the two of them did. The days of work that followed were punctuated by frequent breaks to rehydrate and cool off in the motel's air conditioning.

Even Jasper decided he would rather lounge around inside than out and spent most of the time napping in the temperature controlled indoor portion of his run while they worked. Sadie knew he was probably bored, but with the kennels cleaned both inside and out Sam had torn the creeping vines and weeds out of the outdoor runs in half as much time as it would have taken her to do it, and burned them in a fire pit he uncovered toward the back of the property – they were easily the nicest part of the motel, and it was a convenient way to keep him away from the various cleaning chemicals she and Penny were using to attack the mess inside the motel.

They stayed up late that first day and put together a long list of everything they needed to order before the open house, and as the supplies began to arrive, the reality of opening her own boarding kennel began to set in. Even the basics like pet-safe disinfectant, mops, squeegees, a bulk box of a thousand dog poop bags were exciting to receive. Sam helped her install security cameras in the dog runs so she could keep an eye on her boarding clients remotely, while Penny worked hard to clean the tiles they had discovered under the carpet in the lobby.

Sam's riding mower made short work of the overgrown lawn. It would take a few mow cycles for the grass to look good, but at least it was more presentable. She and Penny discovered the old sign in a ditch and hammered the post back in before putting their new temporary sign up, the words *Sit, Stay,*

Sleep Motel and Boarding standing out proudly in bold. They still needed to work on a logo, but for now, the sign would do.

As soon as they were sure that they would make the deadline, they printed out flyers inviting anyone who wanted to come to their open house on Saturday, and made it clear they were encouraged to bring their dogs, too. They passed the kennel inspection with flying colors on Thursday. On Friday, they put the finishing touches on the lobby and Sadie officially moved into the little apartment above, leaving Room Three to Penny.

By Saturday, they were ready. Sadie woke up early and gave Jasper a bath in the cramped bathroom of her tiny one-bedroom apartment. Most of her things were still in the cardboard boxes that she and Penny had wrestled up the stairs and left in the living room, and she still felt like a stranger in the space, but she could make it feel like home later. With Jasper freshly bathed, she tied a bow to his collar and brushed his teeth before taking him downstairs so he could dry off in his kennel while she changed into the outfit she had carefully selected for the day and took the time to pull her hair back in a neat French braid. She wanted to look professional, but relatable. No one was expecting someone who ran a doggy daycare to wear a business suit, but she didn't want to look like a slob either.

She and Penny were both ready by ten. They met in the lobby, which was nearly unrecognizable. Sunlight streamed in through the windows, and the tile floor shone with how well Penny had polished it. They had torn down the plexiglass fishbowl with Sam's help – and had removed the security completely since it was pointless without the plexiglass – and had given the wooden front desk a polish. They hadn't had time to replace the chairs or update the ancient TV in the corner, but at least the lobby didn't smell like mildew anymore. Penny's laptop was set up on the front desk next to a vase of wildflowers Sadie had gone outside to pick. She just hoped no one would look up. They hadn't had time to replace the stained ceiling panels yet either.

The open house began at eleven, but their first guest arrived early. Elena, the young woman from the grocery store. Sadie had chatted with her a few more times, most recently yesterday when they stopped in to get powdered lemonade mix, cupcakes, and the supplies for hot dogs so they would have something to offer their guests during the open house.

"Wow, this is better than I expected already," she said as Penny ushered her into the lobby. She was carrying a humongous pitcher of something amber colored, which she set on the front desk next to their other drinks and snacks. "I've been hearing people talk about your open house all week and figured you might get more people than you're prepared for, so I figured I'd bring by a batch of my great-grandma's famous sweet tea in case you ran out of the lemonade."

"That's so thoughtful of you," Sadie said. "Thank you. It looks refreshing."

"Go ahead and try some. I might be biased, but I think it's the bes…"

She broke off and turned around as the door to the lobby opened. Sadie recognized Bailey immediately; the woman's cookies had left an impression. Jasper had given the dog version his seal of approval, and the ones intended for humans were some of the best cookies Sadie had ever had. She hadn't spoken to Bailey about selling cookies at the motel yet. Maybe she could do that later today, if the open house went well.

Josh stepped inside right behind Bailey. Neither of them came empty-handed; both had boxes of cookies from Sunshine Desserts. She hadn't expected the people of Greencreek to be so welcoming, but she certainly wasn't going to complain. For the first time, it really hit her that this was her home now. Hers and Penny's. These people weren't just potential clients; they were potential friends.

"I brought cookies! And some for the dogs, too. Josh, can you…" Bailey trailed off as her gaze landed on Elena. Elena glared back at her with such venom that Sadie was shocked Bailey didn't burst into flames on the spot.

"Of course you're here," Elena spit out. "I just can't get away from you, can I? If you won't listen to my apologies, then just leave me be."

Fuming, she brushed past Bailey and Josh and slipped out of the lobby. Bailey hurried to put the box of cookies down on the front desk before hurrying out after the other woman. "Wait, Elena…"

The door shut behind her. Josh handed his box of cookies, which was labeled as for dogs, to Penny and glanced around the room, clearly uncomfortable. "Uh, mind if I go look around?"

"Go ahead," Sadie said. She forced a smile to her face. "It's an open house. Make yourself at home."

He left in a hurry. As the door opened, she heard raised voices from Elena and Bailey but couldn't quite make out what they were saying. She was curious about what the argument was about, but as the door swung shut, she spotted two more vehicles turning into the parking lot. The open house was beginning.

She hurried to fetch Jasper from the back and brought him out front with her to greet people as they arrived. He was a great ambassador for her dog training business and took his job as greeter seriously. She was selfishly glad to find that Bailey and Elena had vanished somewhere. If they were still arguing, at least they were doing so in private. She didn't want anything to go wrong today, not even an argument between two locals.

The morning passed quickly. She and Penny took turns giving tours of the kennels and the one motel room they had managed to get presentable. Their canine guests seemed happy, too. She had filled a small kiddie pool with water in the shaded side of the building to keep them cool, and the dog cookies Bailey had brought were a hit.

When she spotted someone coming down the path to Sam's house a little after noon, she raised a hand in a wave, a smile of greeting already on her face before she realized it wasn't him. The newcomer was an older man she didn't recognize. She felt a pang of disappointment. She hadn't seen Sam all day. She had been hoping he would stop by, if only to witness the fruits of their hard work. Even though he had been helping them clean the place up all week, she hadn't had much of a chance to talk to him yet. He couldn't exactly chat while they were working.

The old man spotted her wave and raised his own hand in greeting, which made her feel obliged to walk over with Jasper and greet him. He focused on the dog first and let Jasper sniff his hands before he scratched the foxhound behind his floppy ears.

"You have a real nice hound here," he said, finally turning his attention to Sadie. "Do you hunt with him?"

"Oh, no," she said. "He was a rescue. I'm a trainer and he's my demo dog. He helps me with lessons and helps me socialize other dogs, that sort of thing."

"At least he has a job. Seen too many hunting dogs go crazy with nothing to do." He extended his hand to her. "Walter Bennington."

Her eyes widened. The name jogged in her memory immediately. This was the man they had bought the motel from.

"Sadie Barton," she said, shaking his hand. "My friend Penny and I are the ones who bought the motel."

"Glad to finally meet you," he said. "It's looking better already. I regret letting it get so bad, but after what happened, I just couldn't bring myself to come back here. That's why I asked Sam if he'd be willing to move in and keep an eye on the place. I didn't want kids breaking in or thrill seekers using it for their videos."

"Well, he certainly did a good job of keeping an eye on it. He nearly gave me and Penny heart attacks when we first got here."

Walter chuckled. "He told me about that. I think he feels bad about giving you a fright, but it sounds like you got things straightened out. Do you mind if I take a look around? I've been wanting to see what you've done to the place."

"We aren't done yet," Sadie warned him. "Not by a long shot. But go ahead and make yourself at home. There are refreshments in the lobby. Oh, and there's a sign-up sheet on the front desk. Our first ten clients get half off boarding, and you can sign either yourself or a friend up if you want."

As he wandered off to explore the motel, she took Jasper to the kiddie pool. A woman with a young lab mix was standing next to the pool with an embarrassed expression on her face as she watched her dog splash in the now-muddy water.

"Sorry, he's obsessed with pools," she said. "Your dog's so well-behaved. What's his name?"

She introduced Jasper to the pair and chatted to

the woman, who gave her name as Beth and her dog's name as Rosco, while she emptied and refilled the pool with cold water, then refreshed the dog bowls next to it.

By the time she finished, she was pretty sure she had not only her first boarding client, but her first training client as well. She felt like she was on cloud nine as she walked back around the building with Beth, intending to offer her and Rosco refreshments from the lobby.

She never got that far. A shriek from someone in the parking lot made her look up in time to see Walter stumble out of Room Ten at the far end of the building. He was clutching his chest and only made it a few steps before he collapsed to his knees on the sidewalk in front of the building.

"He's having a heart attack!" someone shouted. "Call 911!"

Sadie had the presence of mind to pull the lobby door open far enough to usher Jasper inside. Leaving him safely in the building, she raced past the long row of rooms toward Walter. Penny had gotten there first and was clinging to his arm, trying to keep him upright.

"He's babbling something," she said, looking up at Sadie with wide eyes. "He's not making sense."

"Do you have your phone?" She had left hers inside somewhere. When Penny nodded, she crouched next to Walter and said, "I'll take over here. Call for an ambulance. Mr. Bennington? Walter? Can you tell me what's going on?"

"It happened again," he said, reaching up to clutch her arm with enough force to hurt. "He's back, and he killed someone else."

He raised his other hand to point toward the open door to Room Ten. At Penny's terrified look, Sadie rose to her feet. Leaving Walter in her friend's care, she walked toward the open motel room. It should have been locked. They had locked all of the rooms that weren't ready yet, and Room Ten was the worst of them. Now, she couldn't remember whether they had locked it or not. Neither of them had been inside since the first day.

It seemed to take forever for her feet to carry her to the open doorway. She hesitated at the threshold, then stepped inside... only to immediately stumble back out when she saw the body sprawled on the floor where the missing bed used to be.

Elena. The kind grocery store clerk who had come early to their open house to bring them homemade sweet tea was dead, and the scene Sadie saw didn't leave a doubt in her mind that she had been murdered.

CHAPTER SIX

The ambulance took Walter away in a rush, but he was the only one who got to leave for hours after the police arrived. Sadie stood with Penny, watching numbly as the authorities took over the scene. They began questioning the onlookers soon after. Sadie realized with a sickening lurch that whoever killed Elena had been at the open house and might even still be there. She hadn't seen the other woman since she left the lobby shortly before eleven.

She darted a glance toward Bailey, where she was standing in the shade of her delivery van with Josh. Had she been the last one to see Elena alive? Was her kind persona just an act? She wished she knew what the history between the two women was. It was clearly bad, but she had no idea whether it was bad enough to lead to murder.

By the time the sheriff made his way over to them, Sadie and Penny were both sweltering. The sheriff was a tall man with a goatee that made him look like a villain in a bad western and a revolver on his hip that only served to complete the look. He tipped his hat to them as he approached.

"Ladies," he said in a southern drawl so thick she had to wonder if he was putting it on. "I'm Sheriff Islington. Mind if I ask y'all a few questions?"

He started with what happened when Sadie discovered Elena's body and worked all the way back to when the two of them decided to buy the motel. Sadie wasn't sure what that had to do with the murder, but she answered everything she could.

"I'm curious about what exactly led two twenty-something ladies to decide to move from Lexington to somewhere like Greencreek," the sheriff said. "Nothin' wrong with the town, of course, but this area doesn't exactly have much to appeal to city folk."

"We're both twenty-seven," Penny answered. She rubbed her leg as she spoke, though it had been years since the incident with the bus, it still bothered her, and they had been standing for a long time. "And we didn't want to move to Greencreek, exactly. We would have moved just about anywhere for a property as perfect as this one."

Sheriff Islington gave the building behind them a skeptical glance. "You're gonna have to expand on that one for me. I don't think anyone's ever called Bennington's old place perfect, not even the man himself back in its heyday."

"It's perfect for us," Penny insisted. "Between the kennels and the price, it's like it was meant for us."

"Y'all were specifically looking for a motel that came with kennels attached?" He still looked skeptical. Sadie realized with a prickle of disconcert that they might be suspects, not just witnesses. As the two newcomers and the motel's owners, they probably stuck out like sore thumbs.

Penny nodded, but Sadie was the one who spoke up this time. "I know it probably sounds weird, but it's something we've been talking about for years. I'm a dog trainer, and Penny's worked in hotels since she was twenty. We always imagined opening a business together, and we wanted it to be something that played to both of our strengths. A dog motel seemed perfect. We can do boarding and training for the locals, but also do daycare for our guests so they don't have to worry about trying to bring their dogs to every activity or leave them in their room or a hot car.

We talked about it a lot before Penny found the property. It was too perfect to pass up, and we both wanted a change anyway after…"

The sheriff's eyebrows rose so high they almost vanished under the brim of his hat. "Go on," he urged.

Sadie glanced at Penny. She was the one who had been more hurt by what happened, after all. She reached out to give her friend's hand a squeeze. Penny took a deep breath.

"I found out my boyfriend was cheating on me over Christmas," she said. "No, not just cheating… He had a whole other family. A fiancé, kids, all of that. I was the other woman. I just didn't know it."

"He was friends with my boyfriend," Sadie added. "They actually met through us. My boyfriend spent the past two years covering for him and helping him hide his double life from both of us."

"We dumped them both immediately," Penny said. "Jerks. We wanted a change of scenery after that, and then in May, I found this motel online, and well… here we are."

The sheriff chewed on the end of his pen as he looked them over scrutinizingly. "I see. Y'all make a lot of impulsive, life-changing choices?"

"It wasn't impulsive," Penny said quickly.

At the same time, Sadie said, "Not usually, no."

He looked between them and lowered his notebook. "Well, I'd wish you good luck, but you're going to need a darn miracle after this. I'm going to have to ask y'all to clear out for the rest of the day while we get the forensics team in from Atlanta to do their thing. I'll also need access to any security cameras you have on the property. If you need help finding a place to go for the night... well, you can search for other motels as well as my deputies can. You'll find something."

"Are we free to go?" Sadie asked. She glanced at the small crowd of people that were still waiting for their turn to be questioned.

The sheriff followed her gaze. "You're welcome to stick around until everyone else clears out, but I can't let you go in the building, not even to get your things. I'll make sure my deputies get you the necessities before you leave, like your phone and your wallets."

"What about my dog? He's in the lobby. He's probably eaten half of the hot dogs by now."

"He friendly?" At her nod, the sheriff said, "I'll get someone to bring him out to you. In the meantime, sit tight. This is going to take a while."

CHAPTER SEVEN

Their nightmare was just beginning. It didn't really begin to sink in for Sadie until she was on the road, following Penny forty-five minutes away to the motel they were going to stay at overnight. In the back, Jasper was happily unconcerned, napping in her SUV's overpowered air conditioning after his long day of playing host at the open house.

Sadie envied her dog for that. For her part, it was all she could do to keep her eyes on the road and not pull over somewhere to cry. Or scream. She wasn't sure which.

A woman was dead. The brief look she had gotten of Elena's body kept flashing through her mind. Buried under the visceral horror was another type of dread. What was going to happen to the motel now?

Dealing with its bloody past would have been hard enough when the most recent murders took place two years ago, and the killer was behind bars. But now… now it seemed possible that they hadn't even caught the right person.

No one was going to stay at a motel an active serial killer was still haunting.

It was late by the time they finally made it to the other hotel. They didn't talk much when they got there, they just went to bed, Sadie cuddled up with Jasper in one, and Penny clutching a spare pillow in the other. Even with the door locked and the knowledge that no one else on earth knew where the two of them were staying, she kept waking up during the night certain she would see someone standing over her with a knife.

She woke in the morning to the sound of Penny's voice, with Jasper's cold nose snuffling in her ear. Pushing the dog's head away so she could sit up, she saw her friend pacing by the bathroom, her phone pressed to her ear. When she saw that Sadie was up, she gestured at her to wait a moment, thanked the person on the other line, and ended the call.

"That was the Sheriff Islington," she explained as she tossed her phone on the bed. "He said we're free to go back to the motel, though he strongly suggests that we give the whole thing up as a bad idea."

Sadie knew the flare of defiance in her friend's eyes well. "He might be right," she said, even though she already knew what Penny's answer would be.

"No way. We can't give up, especially not now. That's what the monster who killed Elena wants. If we give up now, we're letting him win."

"Or her," Sadie said.

"Huh?"

"I'm just saying… we don't know the killer is a guy."

"I don't think female serial killers are exactly common," Penny said.

Sadie shoved her blankets off and stood up. Jasper danced around her, his whip-like tail whacking the bed frame. "Did you see Elena again after she and Bailey went away somewhere to argue?"

Her friend faltered. "No… I guess I didn't. You really think she did it? She seems so nice."

"I have no idea," Sadie admitted. "It could have been anyone who was there. The only people I know for sure aren't guilty are me and you. Well, and Walter, too. The guy had a heart attack just finding her body. Committing a murder probably would have killed him outright."

"Maybe he was faking," Penny said as she began to pick clothing out of her overnight bag. "If you think about it, it almost makes sense. He's the old owner, so he probably still has copies of the keys, and he'd have been around when the murders happened two years ago as well."

Sadie, who had been reaching for Jasper's leash, faltered. "I'm sure the police would have looked into him back when the murders started."

"Maybe they did, and he framed the guy they arrested to keep them from getting too close." Penny grabbed her bag of toiletries. "Look, I'm not saying I really think that old man killed a bunch of people, but I don't think we should discount anyone at this point. I don't want to give up, but I don't want one of us to end up as the next victim, either. We should install security cameras on more than just the kennels."

"Yeah. Let's swing by the hardware store on the way back and pick some up. I'll ask Sam if he can help us install them."

Penny paused, her hand on the bathroom door as she frowned. "Maybe we should buy a drill and do it ourselves."

"Sam wasn't even at the open house."

"That we know of," Penny said. "He's weird, Sadie. He nearly attacked us with an axe that first day.

I meant it when I said we shouldn't trust anyone, and Sam Walker's at the top of that list."

Sadie pressed her lips together. Maybe her friend had a point, but she had spent more time with Sam than Penny had. Sure, they hadn't exactly been able to chat while they were working on the kennels, but he seemed normal enough to Sadie. Plus, he would have had plenty of chances to hurt them if he wanted to.

And yet… the world was full of the gravestones of women who trusted their guts when they shouldn't have.

"Fine," she muttered. "We'll get a drill when we pick up the security cameras. But you're the one who's going up on the ladder to install them."

Penny rolled her eyes, but she looked relieved as she vanished into the bathroom. Sadie made sure she had her room key, then stepped outside with Jasper. While he sniffed at the narrow strip of grass that bordered the road, she tried not to think about what was waiting for them back at the motel. The police would have taken the body, but she doubted they'd gotten on their hands and knees to scrub the carpets in Room Ten.

The day was just beginning, and they already had a long list of things they had to do. It was far from the triumphant celebration after a successful open house that she had imagined. Penny was determined to see this through, but Sadie's doubts had returned more powerfully than ever. Buying the motel might have been an impulsive mistake but sticking with it after what happened to Elena… that was a choice they were making with their eyes wide open. She just hoped they didn't come to regret it.

CHAPTER EIGHT

Even though they had only been there for a week, they had already become something of regulars at the hardware store. The cluttered, crowded store had supplied everything from paint to polish to cleaning supplies. The best part, at least as far as Sadie was concerned, was that they allowed dogs to come in.

Jasper, who seemed to think that life had turned into one giant vacation, was thrilled to explore the narrow aisles as they gathered what they needed. More security cameras, a drill, and after some discussion, new locks for every single door on the motel.

It was an expensive shopping trip, and they huddled at the end of one of the aisles for a few minutes to discuss how to divvy it up. They were still arguing about it when the electronic bell over the door let out a chirp, and Jasper turned toward the newcomer eagerly, his tail nearly knocking a can of spray paint off the shelf behind him.

Sadie and Penny looked up at the same time, and they both fell silent when they saw Bailey. The young woman looked like a wreck. She made a beeline for the aisle they had just come out of, the one that contained door hardware but paused when she saw them.

"Oh… it's you two," she said. "I thought you left."

"We did," Penny said. "But we came back. We have a motel to run."

"You're really going to keep trying? Even after all of this?"

"We don't have much of a choice," Sadie said, subtly nudging Penny with her elbow. Her friend was glaring at Bailey openly, which seemed like a bad idea if the woman was behind Elena's murder. "We spent everything we had to buy it. Even if we decide to sell, it's going to take a while to get it listed, and we need to make sure we're secure in the meantime."

Bailey glanced into their cart, taking in the security cameras and the heap of new locks. She shuddered.

"I don't know how the two of you can stand to go back there so soon after…" She broke off and swallowed heavily, then changed the subject. "I'm here to pick up a new lock too, for Sunshine Desserts. Josh quit out of the blue this morning when I told him I wasn't planning on opening the store today. He's never been the most reliable employee, but I think he's gone for good this time. I asked for his keys back, and he said he lost them, but I know that's bull because he locked up for me yesterday. I don't think he would do anything, but I don't like that he won't give the keys back, so here I am."

Sadie frowned. Josh had been at the open house too, and he had disappeared at around the same time Bailey and Elena did. Penny was right. They had to treat everyone as a potential suspect.

"Why did he quit?"

Bailey sighed. "He said he's tired of me being an unreliable boss. If you listen to him, then I'm constantly either making him stay late or cutting his hours without warning. I think the truth is he's upset about what happened to Elena, it made him lash out at the first thing that inconvenienced him. Either way, I'm done. I'm not going to have an employee that shouts at me."

"Did he know her?" Sadie asked.

"We both did." Bailey hesitated. "She opened Sunshine Desserts with me four years ago and worked there with Josh and I up until last year. She was my best friend."

"What happened?" Sadie asked. There was still a part of her that wondered if Bailey could be behind the brutal murder, but she couldn't ignore the parallel of two best friends opening a business together. She hoped it wasn't a sign of how things would end for her and Penny.

Bailey shook her head in response. Her eyes brimmed with tears that she swiped away angrily. "She almost killed someone who had an allergy. It was an accident, but she laughed about it afterward, and I just couldn't stand to have her in the shop after that. I don't want to talk about it. I just want to change the store's locks and go home." She took a step away, then paused and looked back. "I think the two of you are crazy for doing this. Just list the motel for sale and go back to where you came from. Nothing good is ever going to come out of that place."

With that ominous warning, she left them alone in their aisle. Sadie exchanged a look with Penny, but they were both keenly aware of Bailey in the next aisle over and neither said a word until they had paid for their purchases and were back outside with their vehicles.

"I'm sorry," Penny said as they loaded their things into the back of her crossover.

"Why?" Sadie asked, surprised.

"This whole thing was my idea. I got us into this mess, and now I don't know how to get us out."

"You couldn't have known what was going to happen. We both read about the murders, and every article we found stated that the killer had been caught and sentenced. Besides, I wanted to do this, too. You didn't force me to sign the title. You didn't make me stay up late every night for two weeks straight coming up with my business plan for the dog kennel. I might have been a little more cautious than you were, but I was all in before this happened."

"And now?" her friend asked.

Sadie hesitated. "Let's see what happens with the case."

It was the best she could offer at the moment. There was a part of her that wanted to run back to Lexington as fast as she could and try to write this nightmare off as a blip while she got back to her normal life, but she knew this might be her one chance to do something more with her life. She couldn't give up on her dreams. Not yet.

She just hoped they didn't end up killing her.

CHAPTER NINE

Sadie was relieved to see the fresh strip of crime scene tape across the door to Room Ten. It meant they didn't have to deal with cleaning it yet. She and Penny checked the other doors to make sure they were still locked, then searched through Room Three, where Penny was staying, and the apartment above the lobby to make sure no one was lying in wait with a knife. Once they determined the motel was safe, Penny stayed in the lobby to begin cleaning up after yesterday's open house, while Sadie took Jasper out back to give him a chance to stretch his legs before she got him settled in his kennel so she could focus on installing the security cameras with her friend.

She had about two seconds of warning when they

rounded the back corner of the kennel wing, and she saw Jasper's body language go from relaxed to excited. She rounded the corner just a step behind him and let out a strangled shriek at the sight of a tall figure that had been waiting just out of sight behind the building. She recognized Sam quickly enough to keep from letting out a full-blown scream, but it was close.

He held his hands out in a placating gesture before reaching into his pocket for a small notebook and pen. She pulled Jasper closer to her, not that he would be helpful if something happened. He was more liable to lick Sam to death than bite him.

"What are you doing here?" she snapped, fear making her tone more unfriendly than it had been since that first day, when he surprised them with the axe. He was already scribbling in his notebook and held it up for her to read after a second.

I heard what happened. Figured I'd keep an eye on the place while you were gone to make sure he didn't come back. Didn't mean to scare you. Again. Sorry.

"What did you expect? A strange guy lurking around the motel right after a murder took place is shady no matter what your excuse is," she muttered.

She wasn't sure why she was bothering to keep

her voice down. Penny would ask Sam to leave if she realized he was here, which was probably the smart thing to do under the circumstances. But despite her friend's distrust, Sadie really didn't think Sam was behind the murder. He scribbled on his notepad for a second, ripped the page off, then wrote another note before holding it up.

I'll leave. But take my number in case he comes back.

He held the ripped off page out to her. She accepted it and glanced at the number before she put it in her pocket. Deciding bluntness wasn't out of place here, she asked, "Do you know who killed her?"

He shook his head.

She chewed on the inside of her lip for a second. Her gut wanted to believe him, but maybe that was just because he had pretty eyes. She no longer trusted her gut or Penny's when it came to men.

"Then you don't know it's a 'he,'" she said at last. "Women can be killers, too."

He raised an eyebrow at her but didn't write anything else. Raising a hand in a wave goodbye, she continued on her way past him with Jasper. Her back prickled when it was turned toward him, but when she finally looked over her shoulder, he was gone.

After getting Jasper settled in his kennel with a

chew toy, the first thing she did was change the lock on the back door, the one Sam had been lurking by, which led into the kennel building. Since the runs were indoor-outdoor, there was the risk that someone could get in through the doggy doors, but those had panels she could lower from the inside to keep the dogs in or out if she wanted to. Those same panels would keep human intruders out or at least slow them down while the cameras alerted her of their presence. To be safe, she lowered all of the panels, even Jasper's. She didn't want him in the outdoor run by himself with a killer on the loose.

Once the kennels were secure, she helped Penny change the rest of the locks. It was repetitive work, but easy enough. The only door they didn't touch was Room Ten. "Did the sheriff say what we should do with it?" she asked as they stood side by side, staring at the door. Even shut, it felt ominous.

"He said they might send someone out later this week to comb through it again, and we should call back next Monday to ask for an update if we don't have one by then."

"Well, I guess we can put it off guilt-free until then," Sadie said, fishing to find the silver lining in the nightmare they were living. "Did you ask him about Walter? Is he all right?"

"Do you think he'd be able to tell us that sort of thing?" Penny asked. "I figured he couldn't share private medical information or whatever."

"That's a good point. I have no idea," Sadie said.

They walked back to the lobby together, where Sadie tucked the garbage from the new locks into the overfull garbage bag Penny had used to clean up the trash from the open house. While Penny went into the laundry room to fetch the little stepladder that had been left behind, Sadie took Sam's number out of her pocket and typed it into her phone. She saved it under his name as a new contact, then typed out a text message to him.

Hey, do you have any idea what happened to Walter Bennington after he went to the hospital? She sent it, then quickly followed up with, *This is Sadie Barton, btw.*

She stared at her phone for a few moments, wondering if that last part had been necessary. Of course it was her. He had given her his number less than two hours ago, and she doubted he knew all that many people who would be texting him from a Lexington area code.

When he didn't answer right away, she worried whether it was strange for her to ask him about Walter. She assumed the two men were on friendly terms. Walter had clearly been visiting Sam right before he came to the open house and had mentioned hiring him to keep an eye on the place. Then she wondered why she was overthinking a simple text message so much and slipped her phone into her pocket, only to withdraw it immediately when it buzzed.

He's fine. I gave him a ride home yesterday evening. Said it was a false alarm.

Penny came out of the laundry room in time to see Sadie smiling at her phone. "I know that look. How on earth did you meet someone already? We've barely left the motel all week, and we're almost always together when we go into town."

"I'm not flirting," Sadie said, rolling her eyes as she slipped the phone back into her pocket. "It was just Sam. He said Walter Bennington is fine, and he's back home already."

"That's a relief," Penny said. "Or maybe a red flag. He could have been faking it. I wish we'd gotten the chance to talk to him face to face before we bought this place. I bet he knows more about the murders than anyone else, even if he wasn't behind them. He lived here while they were happening, after all."

"We should give him a day or two to recover, but then maybe we can see if he'd be willing to talk to us," Sadie said as she grabbed the bag with the security cameras in it. "If we're going to stay here, we need to know what we're dealing with."

CHAPTER TEN

They spent the day continuing their constant battle against the dust, mildew, and stains that had taken over the motel in its two years of disuse and secured the building as best they could. They even toyed with the idea of putting the plywood panels back over some of the windows, but they hadn't been careful when taking them off, and most of the wood was too torn up to reuse.

Neither of them talked about what they were going to do in the long term. They couldn't open like this, not even to take boarding clients. The last thing Sadie wanted was to put someone's beloved pet in danger, and if a killer was targeting the motel, then any living thing that was here might be at risk. She was glued to her phone whenever Jasper was out of sight in his kennel, each incoming buzz a potential warning that someone was snooping around.

But the alert never came. Other than the occasional car that sped past on the highway, the only other person Sadie saw for the rest of the day was Penny.

As evening fell, they microwaved some of the frozen dinners they had stocked up on and ate together in the lobby while Jasper sniffed his way around the edges of the room. Sadie poked at her rubbery pasta with a plastic fork. She had skipped lunch, and she had that shaky feeling of not having eaten enough, but it was hard to feel hungry after everything that had happened.

"Maybe we can start painting some of the other rooms tomorrow," Penny said eventually, when the silence had ticked on for too long. "It'll give us something to do, and it needs to be done either way."

Either way — meaning whether they decided to sell the place or not.

Sadie nodded. "We'll make a run into town tomorrow and stop at the hardware store." She prodded her food and wrinkled her nose. "Maybe we can stop at a restaurant, too, and get something real to eat. I'm going to try to get Walter's number from

Sam, too. I want to talk to him and learn more about what happened two years ago."

"Are you thinking about meeting with him in person?" Penny asked. "It seems risky, but I guess we can't hide out here just the two of us forever, and he is an old man. I bet we could take him. Do you remember seeing any pepper spray for sale at the hardware store? I should get my own."

"I'm sure they do. That place seems to have everything," Sadie said.

It felt good to have some plans, even if none of them were long-term plans. They finished their food and tidied up. After a brief discussion, in which Penny decided she didn't want to sleep alone on the ground floor of the motel with nothing but a thin pane of glass between her and the outside — a very reasonable fear as far as Sadie was concerned — they decided Penny would take the couch in Sadie's apartment, and they would sleep with the door chained and a few of the unpacked boxes propped up in front of it as added security.

Before she went to bed, Sadie made sure the notification volume on her phone was turned up all the way, just in case the security cameras caught motion during the night. The cameras woke her up once during the night, but it was just a raccoon sniffing around the outdoor kennel runs. She lay in her bed with Jasper's head resting on her knee while she watched it until it waddled away, then she flipped through the other cameras until she was satisfied that there were no human intruders on the premises. Still clinging to her phone, she fell back asleep until morning.

She was in the middle of her morning shower when she heard the now familiar chime of the security camera app's notifications. She reached blindly for the phone where she had set it on top of the toilet and held it out of the water spray while she checked the screen. The sight of the words *Person Detected* made her heart skip a beat, and she nearly dropped the phone in her haste to check the video.

They only had two security cameras set up in front of the motel — one over the front door that looked down over the entrance to the lobby and out at the parking lot, and the other at the end of the row of rooms, which would let them see all ten of the doors at one wide angle. It was the camera over the lobby door that had sent the alert. There was a dark red sedan in the parking lot, and a young man standing at the door. It wasn't until he turned his face to glance up at the camera that she recognized him — Josh, Bailey's disgruntled ex-employee.

She watched as he tried to open the lobby's door, then resorted to knocking on it when he found it was locked. Realizing she should go see what he wanted, she shut off the water and dried off, then tapped the microphone button to speak through the camera.

"I'll be down in just a second."

She saw Josh jump on screen. He looked up at the camera again. "That's fine, no hurry," he called out, waving up at her. She made sure the microphone was off before hurrying back into her bedroom. Penny was awake by the time she stepped into the living room, fully dressed, with Jasper by her side.

"What's going on?" her friend asked sleepily.

"Josh from the bakery is here. I'm going to go down with Jasper and see what he wants. And before you ask, yes, I have my pepper spray. Will you come rescue me if I scream?"

"Did you unpack your kitchen knives yet?"

"They're in the box on the counter," Sadie said.

Penny gave her a thumbs up. "Yeah, just shout and I'll come downstairs swinging."

Sadie made her way downstairs with Jasper. She hadn't bothered to put his leash on — she just told him to heel as she approached the lobby door. She pressed a hand to her pocket to make sure her pepper spray was ready to whip out if she needed it, then turned the lock and pulled the door open.

Josh had been leaning against the side of the building. He pushed away from the wall when the door opened and gave her a slightly chagrined smile.

"Sorry about that, I thought you'd be open. I didn't mean to bother you."

"It's no bother at all," Sadie said. She kept the door half open as she stood in the doorway. Jasper leaned against her leg, his weight familiar and reassuring. "How can I help you?"

He scratched the back of his neck. "I was wondering if the two of you were hiring. If you are, I can email you my resume. I have some good references, and I have plenty of experience in customer service work. I've never worked at a hotel before, but I'm a fast learner."

Sadie had been half expecting him to say something about the murder, so it took her a second to process his words. When she did, she blinked and said, "Well, we aren't hiring anyone yet, but if you want to send your resume in anyway, we'll keep it in mind when we're ready." She didn't add that they were no longer even sure they would be opening. She figured it was better to plan for the best-case scenario.

"Are you sure there's nothing you need from me

right now?" Josh asked, taking a step closer. "I can help with cleaning and renovation, too. Whatever you need done, I'm your guy. I really need to land a new job before my rent is due. I had to quit the cookie shop for my own good — Bailey's been acting weird for months, and I didn't feel safe there after what happened to Elena."

"Honestly, we can't afford to hire anyone right now," she said. Hiring Sam had been a one-off, at least for the time being, and they technically hadn't even paid him — they had just given him a free month of rent, which was money they hadn't been planning on getting anyway. She felt a little bad turning him down, but mostly, she was fixated on what he had said about Bailey. "What do you mean you didn't feel safe there?"

He shrugged, not quite meeting her eyes. "She was acting... off, and when I showed up for work the day after the murder, one of the knives in the kitchen was missing. And knowing how much she and Elena hated each other..." He trailed off, then added quickly, "I'm not trying to accuse her of anything."

"Josh, if you think she had something to do with the murder, you should go to the police."

"It's probably nothing." He forced a smile, then

began to turn away. "Thanks anyway. I'll check back in a few weeks in case you change your mind."

She watched him go, unsettled. He had essentially just blamed Elena's murder on Bailey. She didn't know what to do with that information, especially if he didn't want to go to the police. Would they even listen if she showed up to tell them what he had told her? At that point, she would essentially just be spreading gossip.

As he pulled out of the driveway, she shut and locked the lobby door, then reached down to ruffle Jasper's soft ears before turning back toward the door that led up to her apartment. She needed to talk to Penny about this.

She only made it halfway across the room before Jasper turned around, his floppy ears perking up. A moment later, she heard the sound of a car door slam. Someone else was there… or Josh had come back.

CHAPTER ELEVEN

She unlocked the lobby door and peeked outside to see Bailey's white delivery van parked across the parking lot. The woman was already out of the vehicle, striding across the cracked asphalt toward her. Sadie's gut clenched — this was the worst timing imaginable. She should have checked before opening the door. She was tempted to pull back and shut the door in Bailey's face, but the other woman had already seen her and raised a hand in greeting. She had a box of cookies in her other hand. An offering Sadie would have been more tempted to accept if one of the woman's ex-employees hadn't just accused her of murder.

Instead of slamming the door in Bailey's face, she gave her a tight smile and slipped her phone out of her pocket to type a message to Penny. *Bailey's here. Josh thinks she might have killed Elena. Please come down and save me!* With the message sent, she slipped the phone back into her pocket in time to exchange a pleasant greeting with Bailey.

"I'm glad I caught you," the other woman said. "I meant to talk to you about this at the open house but, well..." She trailed off. "That didn't exactly go as planned. I'm always looking to expand the cookie shop, and I'd love to discuss a partnership with you. I've got cookies, and you're going to have guests. It's the perfect match. Who doesn't want to treat themselves to something sweet while they're on vacation?"

Bailey's bright smile felt wrong after the dark accusation Josh had made. This was exactly what Sadie had wanted two days ago, but now she felt like she was swallowing glass as she said, "I'd love to talk, but now isn't really the best time."

"It won't take long. I just wanted to drop off some cookies as a gesture of goodwill and let you know I'm interested. I know what I said at the hardware store was probably rude, and I'm sorry about that. Yesterday was a hard day for me. I think the two of you could turn this place into something good, with enough time. You don't have to make any decisions right now. I totally get that there are probably a lot of things that are up in the air for you."

That was an understatement. Sadie briefly played with the thought of putting her foot down and insisting Bailey leave, but if Josh's accusation held any weight, then making her angry probably wasn't the best idea. Reluctantly, she pulled the door further open and grabbed Jasper's collar so he wouldn't run outside as she stepped back.

"Come on in."

Bailey smiled at her as she walked past and set the box of cookies on the counter. She opened the top and peeked inside, then said, "Oops, these are the dog cookies. I thought I'd leave some samples for you to give to your boarding clients. Completely free of charge on my end, of course. Let me run back to the van to get the other box."

Sadie propped the lobby door open so she could keep an eye on Bailey and make sure she really was coming back with a box of cookies instead of something more deadly, like a knife. Keeping one eye on the door, she peeked inside the box Bailey had left behind. It was a relief to see nothing but some artistically decorated dog cookies inside. Josh had her all sorts of spooked — she had halfway been expecting to see something more gruesome, like a severed hand.

The door that led up to the apartment opened, and Penny came rushing out. She had a knife clutched in her hand, though she quickly tucked it behind her back when she saw that Sadie wasn't currently in the process of being murdered.

"Where is she?" she asked, her eyes darting around the room.

"She had to run back outside to get something," Sadie said. "Quick, hide the knife. I think we should act normal—"

She broke off when Bailey let out a piercing scream.

Jasper raced outside, baying, leaving Sadie no choice but to chase after him. Bailey was standing by the open back of the van. A bundle of white cloth lay on the cracked asphalt in front of her.

"What happened?" Sadie asked. She stumbled to a stop a few feet away from Bailey and managed to snag Jasper's collar. He was still baying at nothing, but he calmed down as she stroked his head. Bailey raised a shaking finger to point at the bundle on the ground.

"It's a knife," she stammered. "I found it tucked under the seat. It… it has blood all over it."

Sadie glanced down, paying closer attention to the white bundle on the ground. She used the toe of her shoe to nudge what turned out to be a dishtowel, to unveil a large kitchen knife stained with dried blood. Penny, who was standing a few feet behind her, gagged and had to turn away. Sadie's mind raced as she looked from the knife to Bailey. It could all be an elaborate setup, but Bailey looked truly shocked. Josh's accusation came back to her, and she swallowed, not sure what to believe.

"Bailey," she said hesitantly. "Do you think there's any chance that Josh might be trying to frame you for Elena's murder?"

Bailey looked at her, uncomprehending. "What are you talking about?"

Penny was giving her a strange look too, but Sadie thought she was onto something. Josh had very plainly hinted that he thought Bailey was behind the murder, which seemed like an odd thing to do if all he wanted was a job. He had been here during the open house, and he knew better than anyone just how strained the relationship between Elena and Bailey was. It was the perfect setup for him to frame her. And using a knife from her kitchen as the murder weapon, then planting it in her delivery van was the icing on the cake.

"Did you hurt Elena?" she asked Bailey directly. With Penny and Jasper on her side and Bailey unarmed, she was willing to take the risk that she was wrong.

Bailey's mouth dropped open. "No, I would never… we fought, yes, and I came close to hating her sometimes, but I didn't want her dead. I swear, I didn't have anything to do with this. This knife is one of mine, but I didn't do this. You have to believe me."

"Then it had to have been Josh," Sadie said. "He was just here, Bailey. You must have passed him on your way in. He was here and he very strongly insinuated that he thought you were behind the murder. He even mentioned this knife. He must have known someone would find it inside your van at some point."

Bailey paled and stared down at the knife. "That's Elena's blood? I don't… Oh my goodness, what do we do?"

"We go to the police," Penny chimed in. She sounded on the verge of panic, and she clutched the small kitchen knife she had taken from upstairs like it was a lifeline. "We bundle that knife back up and we go straight to the sheriff's department. I'm not hanging around here anymore. What if that Josh guy comes back?"

"He's still here," Bailey whispered. "I saw him turn into the driveway next to yours when I got here.

Oh, my goodness, he could be watching us right now."

"Wait, the driveway next to ours?" Sadie said. "That's Sam's driveway."

Penny gave her a look. "Sam can handle himself. He has that axe."

"He doesn't just carry it around with him all day, Penny," Sadie retorted. "What if Josh sneaks up on him?"

Penny grimaced. "Fine. We'll go see if he needs help, but I'm calling the police on the way."

CHAPTER TWELVE

After a hurried discussion, they decided to use a pair of disposable plastic food service gloves from the back of Bailey's van to wrap the knife back up and place it inside the vehicle. Sadie wasn't sure if touching the knife was the right move, but chances were good it was the murder weapon, and it didn't feel right to leave important evidence like that sitting out in the middle of the parking lot where anyone could find it.

With the knife taken care of, she pulled the lobby door open to put Jasper inside. She would have felt a little more secure with him by her side, but she didn't want to risk him getting hurt. She pulled the door shut, then joined Bailey and Penny by the narrow trail that led to Sam's house. Penny was already on the phone, stumbling over her words as she tried to tell the dispatcher what was going on. Bailey had found a big stick somewhere in the tree line and was carrying it like a baseball bat.

Sadie kept an eye on the other woman as they trekked through the tall grass toward Sam's property. She still wasn't sure she trusted her, but she trusted Josh even less. The way he brought up Bailey's 'guilt' felt too forced, especially the way he made a point of mentioning the knife. He had to have been planting the seeds of doubt on purpose. Who knew how many other people he had spoken to about Bailey's supposed odd behavior since the murder?

They paused when they reached Sam's property. It looked peaceful. His truck was parked in the same shady spot as the last time she was here, and the lawn mower was loaded in the back. If she looked down the driveway, she could just spot Josh's car parked at the end of it, almost out of sight. The little yellow house was ominously dark and still. Sadie's stomach twisted. Were they about to walk into another murder scene?

"I don't know if he's armed," Penny hissed into the phone behind her. "Just send help!"

Sadie glanced back at the other two women. Penny was clinging to her phone, and Bailey looked like she was on the verge of either running away or fainting, though she kept a death grip on her branch. Sadie's heart raced in her chest. She had her pepper spray in her hand and was ready to use it if she needed to, though she was trying not to think about how long she had been carrying it around in her purse. Did pepper spray go bad?

She started moving towards Sam's house and heard the other two women follow her. Usually, Penny was the one at the front of whatever they did, but as much as she loved her best friend, she knew Penny's weaknesses as well as her own. Penny wasn't good at confrontation. Sadie was always the one to stand up for both of them, though the last time they had been in any danger of actual physical harm had been back when they faced down a bully in middle school.

This was different.

Penny stuck close to her back as she climbed the porch steps. She was still on the phone with the dispatcher, but she had gone quiet. All Sadie could hear was three sets of breaths, each one coming too fast. And then... footsteps. She froze and raised the pepper spray, her finger on the trigger. If Josh opened the door, he wouldn't know what hit him.

The knob turned. The door swung open — and

Sam stared out at them. Her finger twitched on the pepper spray, but by some stroke of luck, she managed to avoid spraying him. She lowered her arm, feeling Penny reach out and grab her elbow for support. Sam looked uninjured, but judging from the way his hand froze on the door as he stared out at them, he was more than a little concerned to find three armed women on his porch. Moving with cautious slowness, he shut the door in her face. She heard the thud of the deadbolt settling into place.

"Sam, wait!" She stepped forward to pound on the door. She was on her third or fourth strike when she heard the deadbolt turn and the door opened. She took a step back as Sam came out, this time with his notebook and pen. He had already written something and turned it toward her now. She saw three question marks in the center of the page and nothing else.

"Is Josh here?" Sadie asked. She saw him glance at the pepper spray and tucked her hand behind her back. He raised an eyebrow and shook his head.

"Oh, thank goodness," Penny breathed behind her. She turned away to tell the dispatcher what was going on. Bailey backed off too, glancing toward the driveway. Josh's car was a little more visible from this angle, but they could only see the back of it. Sadie couldn't tell whether he was in it or not.

She heard the rustle of paper. When she looked back, Sam had written another note. *What's going on? Whose car is that?*

"Josh's." She realized she didn't know his last name, so she added, "He works at the cookie shop. Worked, I guess. He quit. And we think he killed Elena and is trying to frame Bailey."

Sam's expression oozed skepticism. He raised his notepad to write something else. In her pocket, Sadie's phone chimed with the now-familiar notification from the security camera app. Her stomach dropped and she fished the phone out of her pocket. The *Person Detected* notification didn't even surprise her. All she felt was dread as she pulled up the live feed.

She saw Josh on foot in the parking lot. He must have parked in Sam's driveway and then walked back over to the motel undetected. As she watched, he peeked in the van's windows, then walked around to the back to open the rear doors. She saw him look down at the knife where it lay in the back of the delivery van for a long moment before he turned to glance around the parking lot, as if looking for witnesses. He stared directly at the camera for a second before he turned back to the van, reached inside, and withdrew the knife. Then he shut the van doors quietly and turned toward the building.

The building where Jasper was currently waiting for her to come back.

Her phone slipped from her fingers as she turned away from Sam and ran down the porch steps, ignoring Bailey's alarmed squeak and Penny's, "Wait, Sadie!" as she ran back down the path between Sam's house and the motel. She wasn't a runner. Try as she might, the habit never stuck, but today her feet flew down the path so fast she felt like an Olympic sprinter. Josh had vanished by the time she made it to the parking lot. She didn't waste time looking for him, she just raced straight for the lobby door and threw it open, holding the canister of pepper spray in front of her like it was a shield.

Jasper darted out and danced around her legs, his pink tongue hanging out of the side of his mouth as he panted happily, probably wondering what had her so excited.

"Oh, Jasper." She dropped to her knees and threw her arms around the dog. He licked her cheek, then gave a quiet woof and pulled away. She looked up to see Sam right behind her. She hadn't even realized he had followed her. He dropped a hand to pat Jasper's head almost automatically as the dog approached him.

Behind him, Penny and Bailey stumbled out of the overgrown path. Sadie rose to her feet, feeling a prickle of unease now that she knew Jasper was all right.

"Where's—" she started, but Sam shook his head, pressing a finger to his lips in the universal sign for *quiet*, then pointed toward the end of the row of rooms toward Room Ten. Sadie glanced down at his other hand, where he held her phone, the security camera feed still playing on the screen.

He must have seen where Josh went, she realized with a jolt. By some stroke of luck, he had decided to revisit the murder scene instead of going into the lobby where she had left Jasper. It was the only room whose lock they hadn't changed. She hadn't even checked to see if the police had locked it when they left. Now that she thought about it, they probably hadn't. It wasn't as if they had keys to the motel and these doors didn't lock automatically. As Penny and Bailey hurried toward them, she mirrored Sam's silent gesture to be quiet, then whispered, "He's in Room Ten."

"The police are almost here," Penny whispered back. "What should we do?"

"Does the room have a back exit?" Bailey asked.

Sadie shook her head, immediately seeing what

Bailey was getting at. The only way out of the room was the door or the window, both of which were on front of the building. Josh only had one way out.

"We could block him in," she whispered. "Make sure he can't leave until the police get here."

"The door opens in," Penny hissed. "How are we supposed to block it?"

"We could pull the van up really close to the building," she said, her mind racing as she stared at the delivery van. It wasn't one of the huge ones that towered over everything. It was small and compact, and low to the ground. If they parked it right in front of the room, Josh would still be able to open the door, but he wouldn't be able to go anywhere unless he managed to climb over the van. It didn't have enough clearance for him to crawl underneath. At least… she didn't think so. "It would block him in until the police get here."

"I can't believe this is happening," Bailey murmured. "But all right. Let's do it."

They all stood back as Bailey climbed into the van and started the engine. It was a quiet vehicle, but there was no way Josh wouldn't hear it anyway. Sadie, Penny, and Sam all stood back and watched with bated breath as Bailey slowly backed the delivery van out of its spot and pulled forward toward the end of the row of rooms. With no overhang, there was plenty of space for her to maneuver onto the sidewalk. She got so close to the side of the building that the van's mirror scraped the wall. Sadie saw the door to Room Ten open just before the van passed in front of it. Josh peeked out, then jumped back with an oath as the van blocked the exit. Almost immediately, he pounded on the side of the vehicle.

"Bailey! What gives? What are you doing?"

Bailey hopped out of the van on the passenger side and walked around to the back so she could talk to Josh face to face through the six-inch-wide gap between the van and the building. "We're keeping you in there so you can't hurt anyone else, Josh. I know what you did to Elena. I found the knife."

"What knife?"

Sadie and the others joined Bailey. Josh peered out at the four of them — five, if Jasper counted. He was wearing an uncertain smile, but Sadie could see the sweat beading at his temples. She didn't think it had anything to do with the temperature.

"I saw you take it out of the back of the van," she said. "I was watching on the cameras."

"Oh, that?" he chuckled, raising an arm to prop himself up against the van in an effort that Sadie guessed was intended to make him look casual. "I was just—"

"Save it, Josh," Bailey snapped. "I should have known it was you even before I found the knife! You were obsessed with the original killer. It was all you talked about for months after the murders. And you were always watching those true crime shows on your phone. You even asked me how I'd get away with murder if I had to! I just want to know why. Why kill her?"

Josh laughed, though the sound was more confused than amused. "Why do you care? You two hated each other anyway."

"I was mad at her. That doesn't mean I wanted her dead." Bailey's voice broke on the last word. "Just… why? Enough lying. The police will be here soon, and we're going to tell them everything. You have the murder weapon on you. You hid your car in Sam's driveway and sneaked back over here to lurk at the scene of the murder. You're not going to fool the police. I just want to know why. This is the only chance you'll get to tell your story, Josh."

Josh was silent for a long moment. When he finally spoke, his entire demeanor shifted. He sounded and looked colder, with no more pretending to be anything he wasn't.

"You want to know why?" he asked. "Because I wanted to know what it felt like to kill someone, and she was convenient. I thought I could get away with it if I made it look like you did it. I hoped it would make the news — a copycat crime two years after that string of murders should have been newsworthy. I thought the idea of working here after what I did was funny. If it all worked out, I could have killed another person every couple of years and kept the legend alive." He kicked the van. "But you had to go and wreck all of that, Bailey. That's just like you. Working for you was a drag, I hope you know that. You suck the fun out of everything."

He kicked the van again, then began struggling to get out of the room in earnest when the sound of sirens reached them. Sadie stepped forward at the same time Penny did, and they pulled Bailey into a hug together, leaving Sam to hold Jasper's leash as the police pulled into the parking lot.

EPILOGUE

Sadie rolled a ball across the lobby floor. Jasper bounded after it, slipping and sliding on the tile before he snatched it up. He trotted around the room with it held in his mouth, his tail wagging proudly. She leaned back against the rolling chair with a sigh. Across the room, sitting in one of the uncomfortable waiting chairs, Penny was scrolling through social media on her phone, occasionally pausing to update Sadie on something one of their mutual friends had posted.

When Sadie's phone chimed, they both perked up.

"Who is it?" Penny asked. "Did we get a booking?"

"It's just Sam," Sadie said as she opened the message.

"Oh." Penny slouched again. "You're sure there haven't been any new emails?"

"I've been checking three times an hour, and we both have our notifications set to max volume," Sadie said. "We'd know if we had gotten any."

They shared a silent look before Sadie returned to Sam's text message. It had been a week since Josh's arrest, and while they had been marketing their boarding and dog training services, they hadn't had any luck so far.

Sam's message was a continuation of an earlier conversation. He had offered to keep up the motel's lawn regularly. Sadie knew they couldn't afford to pay him, but they couldn't afford to buy their own lawnmower either.

I have an old push mower you can borrow, his newest message read. *If you won't let me use the riding mower. Seeing the grass that long is physically painful.*

She snorted. Sam's main source of income was a lawn care business, and he seemed to be more passionate about the work than she had expected. *Fine,* she typed back. *We don't have much of a choice but to accept. We're paying you back when we can, though.*

He sent back a smiling face emoji. She put her

phone down with a sigh. It might take a while before they could pay him back even for something as simple as an old push mower. She didn't know how long they could keep this up until they had to talk seriously about selling the motel, even though the thought put a lump in her throat. She didn't want to give up on things before they even really tried.

Jasper perked his head up and looked towards the door, the ball slipping out of his mouth to bounce away across the room.

Both women straightened up. Sadie heard a car door slam shut. She felt a moment's unease but then told herself she was being ridiculous. Josh had been arrested. The danger was gone.

She called Jasper over just as the door to the lobby opened, letting Beth in. The kind older woman from the open house looked between Sadie and Penny, then smiled down at Jasper.

"Hi, there," she said. "It's me again. Are you open for business?"

"Yeah, we're open," Sadie said, excited. "Well, we're taking boarding and training clients. The motel rooms aren't open just yet."

"Oh, that's fine. I need somewhere to board Rosco. I'm going out of town this weekend, and I don't have anyone else to watch him."

"We'd love to take him," Sadie said. She tapped the space bar on Penny's old laptop repeatedly to wake the screen up in order to load their booking software — the cheapest they could get.

"Oh, wonderful," Beth said, her expression relaxing. "That's such a relief. What all do you need from me?"

"I'll need his vaccine record first. He needs to be current on rabies, DHPP, and Bordetella," Sadie said. "We'll ask you to pay a deposit up front, then the rest when you come to pick him up. Does he have any allergies or medical conditions we should know about?"

Her fingers flew over the keyboard as she typed Rosco's information in, her heart galloping as Penny watched from across the room, sitting on the edge of her seat. Beth and Rosco were their first clients. The first, Sadie hoped, of many. A single dog booked for a weekend stay wasn't much, but it was a start.

Printed in Dunstable, United Kingdom